ARABELLA'S VICTORIAN SCHOOL DAY

BY SUE HUBAND

Introduction

Hello. I'm Arabella Twigg. You may remember me, or you may not know me at all. I'm the quiet, boring one who sits by herself in class. The other girls think I'm funny. I don't blame them, it's probably my clothes, and my hair. I mean, who wears their hair in two plaits tied with enormous ribbons at the ends these days? Exactly. Unfortunately my Mum chooses my clothes too, so you can imagine. Don't get me wrong, I love my Mum, but she does make me wear the most horrendous things. I've tried telling her, after all, I'm nearly nine.

Mind you, her cooking's much the same as her choice in clothes. She has this strange idea that food should be bright and colourful, regardless of whether the ingredients actually go together. She loves making things up, mostly stuff we can't eat. This means me, my horrid brother, Tom and my Dad, Stanley, who, we rarely see, have to pretend to enjoy it.

I should point out that the reason we don't see much of Dad is because he's busy inventing things in his laboratory, it's really the shed in the garden, but he gets cross when we say that. I have to tell you that we haven't actually seen anything he's made. His latest invention, a washing-up machine, managed to smash all the

plates in the house, and his vacuum cleaner that runs on ,
an awful sticky mess everywhere. I'm surprised that Mum doesn't
get mad at him, but she says it keeps him happy. Honestly, that's
grown-ups for you.

And then there's Gran. I suppose you could say she's my
favourite in the whole world. I know she's a bit odd, but she loves
me. I visit her a lot in her little house, it's really the garage, but
Mum says she's safer there. I often go in to help her. She makes
her own clothes and perhaps they are a bit unusual. The thing is,
she makes them out of any old bits and pieces she can find,
curtains, bedspreads, blankets, plastic bin liners, anything, and
then she decorates them with other stuff, like feathers, buttons, old
leaves. She's quite creative actually.

I know that some people think we're a bit odd and I suppose
we are, really. I must be the most boring one of the family, well, I
am, except that lately, strange things have happened to me.

The other day, for instance, it was a normal school day
morning, I was getting ready for school and I was late as usual.

3

Chapter 1

'Come on, you two,' Mum called upstairs,' You're going to be late for school again.'

'Be down in a sec', Mum'. I shouted back. I didn't hear anything from Tom's room, but I never wait for him anyway. He doesn't like his mates to see me with him, but that doesn't bother me. They're always in trouble.

I grab my two homework books and my pencil case and throw them in my bag. I'm glad I haven't got to give this work in 'til Friday, because I haven't a clue what to write about a Victorian School Day. We were supposed to be going on a trip where we visit a Victorian classroom and dress up and everything, but it had to be cancelled at the last minute. Mrs. Osborne, my class teacher got 'flu or the cat died or something. So we couldn't go. It's a shame because we were all looking forward to it and instead we had to watch this video about it. I couldn't see the screen very well because I got pushed to the back and I'm not very tall and I must have nodded off. Anyway, I'll have to think of something to write.

I run downstairs and find Mum in the kitchen. She's making my sandwiches. I wonder what I've got today.

'Come along and have your cereal,' said Mum. 'I've made some fresh muesli. I know you like it.' I look down into the bowl. It looks like rabbit food or the contents of the vacuum cleaner bag, and it probably tastes like it too.

'Here's the milk,' said Mum. I pour the milk on to this dusty mess and some of the dust rises to the surface and sits on the top. I can't possibly eat this.

'Thanks, Mum, but would you mind if I just had a banana? You know how much I love bananas.'

'Well, of course, dear, if that's what you'd like. You do seem to eat quite a lot of them lately. But I do worry if that's enough for you. I don't want you to lose weight and turn into one of those anarchic people.'

'I think you mean anorexic people, Mum.'

'Well, whatever.'

I don't want to tell her that Gran keeps me well supplied with proper food. She knows about Mum's cooking, you see. Mum is chopping the top off a pineapple and cutting it into slices, but she's leaving all the rough skin on round the edge. I do believe she's making pineapple and fish-paste sandwiches. How disgusting is that?

Just as I start peeling my banana, the kitchen door opens and Gran walks in. She's wearing an old army blanket with yellow dusters and white handkerchiefs stitched on to it in odd places.

'Good morning, Ivy, 'morning Arabella,' and then, seeing me eating a banana, whispers in my ear,' Oh dear, was it muesli again?'

'Morning, Gran,' and give her a conspiratorial wink.

'Morning, Mum. How are you? You're looking very... very....' she's struggling for the right word, I can tell.

'Very hot in that dress'.

'Oh, do you like it? I was turning out one of the drawers the other day and I found a packet of new handkerchiefs and a packet of yellow dusters and I thought they'd be just the thing to brighten up this dress. Oh, I see you're having pineapple.'

She leans over to the waste bin and picks out the top of the pineapple. 'You're not going to throw this away, are you? It's just the thing for the top of my latest hat. Just what I've been looking for.'

Mum is dumbstruck, but manages to whisper, 'Of course, help yourself.'

I finish my banana and run upstairs to clean my teeth. By the time I get back downstairs again, Gran is lifting the banana skin out of the bin.

'Waste not, want not, I always say,' said Gran. 'Anyway, how's school, Arabella?'

'Fine thanks, Gran, but I must run, I'm late as it is. When I get back, I'll come and see you, alright?'

'Lovely, my dear. I shall look forward to it.'

'You know, I'm only in the way here, when Dad's experimenting,' I whisper to Gran.' He's only going to be filling the place with bubbles. It's his latest development, a bubble machine. Though why anyone would want such a thing beats me.'

'I'll see you later then. Come and give your old Gran a kiss before you go.' I bend to give her a kiss and I'm swept up into this enormous blanket. How she doesn't fry in that thing, I'll never know. I manage to struggle free.

'Sorry Gran, must run. See you later.'

'Here, don't forget your sandwiches,' said Mum, as she pushes my lunch box into my hands. As if I could forget them. I race out before she gives me anything else to eat.

Chapter 2

I'm rushing down the corridor, trying to stop everything from falling out of my bag and fasten my cardigan at the same time. Why am I always in a rush? I never seem to be on time no matter how early I get up in the morning. In my head I can hear Mrs. Osborne saying 'you're late AGAIN, Arabella. You really must ask your mother to buy you an alarm clock for Christmas'. She doesn't realise that if I said that, my father would probably have to invent one and goodness only knows what that would look like. That's strange.

Everything seems very quiet. Usually I can hear noises coming from the other classrooms. The corridor is very dark today and I'm sure there were loads of posters on the walls. These walls are bare. And the windows, they're very high up and have tiny panes of glass, no wonder it's so dark. I can hear my shoes on the stone floor. Wait a minute, we have carpet on the floors in our school. Where am I?

I find the door to what I think is my classroom and knock gently. A booming voice shouts back, 'Come'. That's definitely not Mrs. Osborne. Opening the door, I walk in to a very different classroom. This isn't my classroom. I'm standing in a Victorian schoolroom, just like the ones in our text-books.

Heavy wooden, iron-framed desks are formed into rows and children are busily working. None of them lifts their head to look at me. That's odd. When anyone new comes into our class, we all want to see who it is. These children hardly move. And then I see the reason why.

A tall, thin man, wearing a black gown is moving towards me and he's waving a rather nasty looking cane in his hand. The look on his face is even nastier.

'And who might you be, coming into my class at this late hour?' he roars, pushing a very sharp nose close to my face.

'Please, sir, I'm Arabella Twigg, sir. I'm so sorry I'm late. Mrs. Osborne is used to me being late, sir. I'm very sorry.'

'SORRY, Sorry,' he roars. ' How dare you? And whoever this Mrs. Osborne might be, I don't tolerate lateness in my school. In future, Arabella Twigg, you will be here on time or face the consequences. Now you will accept your punishment. Hold out your hand.'

I'm too shocked and frightened to argue. Besides, he didn't look the sort of man who would like anyone to question him. So, meekly, I put down my bag and hold out my hand. Before I can take a breath, this frightening person has whacked me on the hand three times with his willowy cane. It really hurt but I'm determined not to cry.

'Now go to your seat and get on with your work.'

With tears stinging my eyes, I try to look for an empty seat. I walk down the nearest row and the only space I can see is a double desk at the back. A scruffy-looking boy is sitting at one desk, but he slides across the seat to make room for me.

'Shhh... don't let 'im 'ear you or 'e'll belt you again. He's a cruel s... sorry... well, 'e is. You want to watch yerself. Yer sitting in a boys' line, but never mind. I'm Tom, by the way. I'll sort you out later. Now keep yer 'ead down.'

'Thanks, Tom.'

Tom pushes a slate and a sort of pencil in front of me, then points to the rows of sums on the board. I only hope I can do them. I want to stay out of trouble, but I can't help thinking that won't be easy.

It seems like ages later, but I don't suppose it is really, when the schoolmaster calls out. 'Pencils down. Heads up. Time for drill.' I look around at the other children looking for a clue to what he means. I've never heard of drill, except when we have a fire drill at school, and I'm pretty sure he doesn't mean that.

I think the boy next to me, Tom, must realise I'm confused, because he leans across and whispers, 'This is where we goes out into the yard for exercise. Yer 'as to go wiv the girls with the class monitor. She's one of the older girls and she teaches the younger ones. Watch what the over girls do and do the same. Yer'll be alright.'

'We'm goin' wiv Mr. Willerby in the boys' yard, wus luck.' I nod my head gratefully. I'm so glad he's decided to be my friend. After all, he doesn't know me and just talking to me could land him in trouble.

'Thanks. Er.. Tom,' I whisper,' what's his name again?'

'Oh dear, you don't know anythin', do yer? That's Mr. Willerby. 'E's cruel and 'ard 'e is. You 'as to watch yerself wiv 'im.' Looking around the classroom, it's obvious that some of their mothers don't wash in a popular soap powder, in fact, judging by the array of greyish clothing, I think it's unlikely that they wash at all. I mustn't be unkind, though, and I must remember that washing powders haven't been invented yet.

'Line up', comes the command and everyone takes their place by the door, one behind the other. It's strange because the girls are in one line and the boys in another. We all line up together and we have P.E altogether, but here, boys and girls even have separate playgrounds and separate entrances. How weird is that? A girl appears. She's not much older than me. She must be the monitor who takes us for drill. I'm standing at the back of the line, hoping that she won't notice me.

'Ready, quick march,' shouts Mr. Willerby, looking more like an ugly black crow than a schoolteacher. 'Left, right, left, right, at the double. Keep together. Jenkins, watch what you're doing, stupid boy.' Poor Jenkins turns bright red and struggles to get in step. I feel sorry for him. I always struggle with left and right.

Outside we go, out into this awful bare yard. There's not a tree or a plant in sight. A high, stone wall with iron railings surrounds it. There's even spikes on top of the railings. It's more like a prison than a school. And Mr. Willerby is more like a gaoler than a teacher. No wonder the children are terrified to speak. I can't imagine how my brother Tom would fit in here. He'd be beaten every day. Mine you, he's so horrid, I wouldn't mind him being punished occasionally. It might teach him a lesson.

The drill session lasts about fifteen minutes. The girl monitor isn't as strict as Mr. Willerby, but we have to swing our arms about and jump up and down. It's a bit like you see soldiers doing on the parade ground. The difference is that they're fit and I'm not. So by the end of it I'm puffing and blowing and I've got a face the colour of a beetroot. I'm almost relieved when the monitor gives the order to return to the classroom. I'm looking forward to break–time, but I'm soon disappointed to find that the drill session WAS our break and it's heads down again for handwriting. Dinner-time is some way off.

Chapter 3.

I shouldn't complain about my Mum's sandwiches. After all, some of the children in the class only had a piece of dry bread for their lunch. The lucky ones had a piece of cheese. Tom even had an apple, but when I asked him if they had an apple tree, he seemed a bit shy about telling me where he'd got it from. I wouldn't blame him, though, because he's so thin and he's probably starving most of the time. His clothes look clean but quite old, so they probably don't have much money. Anyway, he's been kind to me and that means a lot.

At the end of the school day, Tom offers to take me home with him. I don't seem to have many options, so I'm very grateful.

'We ain't got much, though, but I'll see yer alright. My Mum's good wiv strangers. She'll 'elp anybody out and seein' as 'ow you ain't got nowhere to go, you best come wiv me.'

'That's very good of you, Tom, if you're sure your Mum won't mind. It's a bit difficult for me, you see, because I don't really belong here. I don't really know how to explain it, but, one minute I was in my own school and the next, I was here.'

I can tell by the puzzled look on Tom's face that he doesn't understand what I'm saying.

'Well... wherever yer've come from, yer 'ere now, ain't yer? And seein' as 'ow you ain't got nowhere else to go, yer comin' wiv me. But you ain't told me yer name 'ave yer?'

'My name's Arabella, Arabella Twigg, but you can call me 'Bella. It's easier to remember.'

'Well. Come on, 'Bella, we'd best get going, or Mum'll think I'm in trouble wiv the law agen.'

We leave the schoolyard and walk along a road, busy with shops and several horse-drawn carts rumbling by. This must be the centre of a village.

'There's quite a lot happening here, Tom.'

'This is called the Bullring. I've never seen any bulls 'ere, but I 'spose there was once. I didn't want to tek you the other road, 'cos we 'as to go past The Swan. It's a bit quicker that road, but me Dad might be in the pub and if 'e sees me, 'e's bound to give me an errand or summat. Ony road, this way you gets to see a bit more of the village.'

'It's a nice place, Tom. Do you like living here?'

'Never bin anywhere else. They tell us that they 'ave 'Whizzers and Screws, that's pickpockets and burglers, in the big cities like London. So I 'spose we're lucky. Mind -there's a coach goes between Wolver'ampton and Dudley, called the Miller's coach, I ain't never bin on it, but they say they 'as 'ighway robbers along the old coach road. The coaches stop off at the 'Court 'ouse' over there.'

Tom points to a double-fronted building behind the church. It's obviously a public house, but I suppose they must have held the court hearings there as well. It sounds quite exciting travelling by horse-drawn coach, but the thought of highway robbery is pretty scary.

'This way,' said Tom, as we turn left in front of the churchyard. 'We could 'ave walked out of the school right past the front of the church, but like I say, we might 'ave met me Dad. The men are gettin' ready for the Wake next wik. They're practicin' drinkin' already. Mind you, they've all bin workin' real 'ard wiv' the nails, so I 'spose they deserve a bit o' fun.'

I'm not sure what he means by 'busy wiv,I mean with,the nails, but I don't want to keep asking too many questions. As we walk along, Tom explains that the Sedgley Wake is an annual festival celebrated at the beginning of November, following All Saint's Day. A lot of people have their weddings in this week because nobody works. People spend their time eating and drinking and visiting friends and family. Sporting events are organised too and everyone joins in the fun. Tom says that some people forget Easter or Whitsuntide, but no one forgets the Wake. We turn a corner and pass a row of small, stone cottages. On the opposite side of the road, I notice a smaller building with bars at the window.

'What's that building, Tom? It's not a house is it?'

'No, that's the nail shop. People in the village meke nails, see and when they've med 'um, they brings um 'ere to sell. This'n owned by Wilkes and Jordan, but we allis teks ours to 'The Widow'.'

'The Widow?'

''Er names Eliza Tinsley, but everyone calls her 'The Widow'. Ony road we best get a move on or Mum'll think I'm scrumpin' agen'.

As we're walking downhill there's green fields between the rows of cottages. I can see more farmland below us. The few cottages I can see have small gardens. Suddenly Tom stops outside one of the tiny stone cottages. ''Ere we are then. It's not much but it's 'ome and me Mom'll mek you welcome. Come on in.'

Even Tom has to bend down to open the door to this tiny cottage. We walk straight into a room that is a living room and a kitchen. A delicious smell of cooking meets us and steam is rising from a big pot sitting on top of the black stove. A kettle hangs from a hook above the range and two small children, a boy and a girl, are dangerously near the hot stove.

'I hope you two are not playing near the stove,' came a voice from outside.

'It's alright, Mom, I'm back now. I'll keep an eye on 'em. Come on, you two, you 'eard what Mom said. Move back from the grate.' Two small, rather grubby faces looked up at Tom.

'Who's that?' said the boy boldly, pointing at me.

'Don't be so rude. Where's yer manners? This is Bella. She's a friend from school.'

'Is she yer girlfriend?' asked the little girl, with a cheeky grin.

'No, she ain't and I'll learn yer to mind yer manners as well. Yer cheeky little varmint.'

'Mom don't know she's comin', does she? She'll give yer a clout when she sees 'er.' I'm beginning to feel uncomfortable. I shouldn't have come.

'Look, perhaps I should go. It was very kind of you to bring me here, but I don't want to cause any bother, really I don't.'

'Don't get frettin'. Take no notice of these pair. Proper little trouble mekers they are. They're twins but not so you'd know it, bein' a boy and a girl and all. That's 'Enry and that's Alice. Now you two, say 'allo to Bella.'

They seem reluctant to do as they're told, so I thought I'd help them out a bit. I remember the times my Mum told me to speak to some new people. I always clammed up, unable to say a word.

I bent down to the twins and held out my hand. 'Pleased to meet you, I'm Bella.' They just stared at my hand. The look on their faces convinced me that they thought I'd obviously come from another planet. But then, I suppose, to them I might well have.

We're spared any more awkward conversation because the back door opens and in comes Tom's Mum carrying a basket of wet washing. She's quite small and thin with light brown hair escaping from a sort of bun. Her dull brown dress is almost covered by a huge apron. She looks extremely hot and very tired.

'Oh, there you are. I didn't hear you come in, but then you usually come in round the back. What brings you coming in the front door?' Tom's Mum closes the back door behind her and turns and sees me.

'Oh.. I see.. I'm sorry love. I didn't know we'd got a visitor.'

'Look, I'm the one who should be sorry, coming like this.'

'Not at all, my dear. It's just I didn't hear Tom come in, that's all. I was out in the wash-house and what with the boiler on the go. You'll have to excuse the mess, it's wash day, you see and I'm a bit behind. Make yourself at home, dear. Tom, make yourself useful and make the girl a cup of tea while I hang this last bit of washing up.'

Tom hasn't introduced me to his mother, but I suppose she must be Mrs. Smith. I have to say, seeing her with all that washing, I can't help thinking how much easier washing day is in our house. We don't have to heat the water in a boiler outside in a wash-house, or man handle piles of wet washing. We just put ours in the washing machine and the machine does the rest. Except the washing machine my father invented of course.

'You must have loads of washing to do with a husband and three children, Mrs. Smith. I bet they keep you busy,' I said, trying to think of something to say.

'That's not the half of it, my dear. Hasn't Tom told you? He's got another sister and two more brothers, only they're out working, thank the Lord.'

I didn't want to seem rude, but looking around this tiny cottage, it's impossible to think that a family of eight can actually live here. I don't know how many bedrooms they have, but from by the size of the cottage downstairs, I don't think it can have many. Mrs. Smith must be a real wonder. Everywhere is so clean and tidy and, judging by the lovely smell coming from the cooking pot, she does her best to put food on the table. It can't be easy because they probably don't get paid much for the nails they make. I'll have to ask Tom all about the nails later. I can't help wondering how my Mum would manage with all these people to look after in such a small house with very little money. Most of the girls in my class go with their mums to M&S. for their food, just imagine how expensive that must be. They don't have M&S here, or anything like it.

Mrs. Smith is very friendly and motherly. She keeps smiling at me, even though she must be very tired.

'Come along, my dear. You can help me lay the table. It's not much of a meal, I'm afraid, but you're very welcome.' Looking at Tom's Mum, I feel as if I've been wrapped in a cuddly blanket, a bit like Gran's blanket dress. I'm happy to be here with Tom and his family.

Chapter 4

We ate our tea before Mr. Smith came home. Tom's Mum said it would be easier because there wouldn't be room around the table for everyone when the others came back from work. Tom explained that his two older brothers, Jack, who is thirteen and Albert, who is fifteen, both work up at the Hall. They're labourers on the estate farm, just like his Dad used to do until his accident. They didn't say what had happened to him and I didn't like to ask. Apparently the cottage belongs to the big estate as well and they rent it. It's called a tied cottage. That means they can only live here while the family works for the estate. His sister, Emma, works in the big house. I think she's a sort of maid. I can't help wondering what will happen to the family if any of them get married and move away. Will they have to leave this little cottage?

I must say that the stew Tom's Mum gave us was absolutely delicious. It was full of vegetables and small pieces of meat. Tom says that they grow some vegetables in a small back garden. They keep a few chickens too. They used to have a pig, but it had to be slaughtered for meat. I wouldn't be surprised if the meat in the stew came from that pig. I know we don't like to think of animals being killed for food, but when you've got such a big family to feed

I suppose it's necessary. Anyway, it tasted lovely. Mrs. Smith is a very good cook and a very clever lady. I wish my Mum could cook like Mrs.Smith.

After we'd eaten we help clear away and lay the table for the others, Tom suggests we go for a walk before it gets too dark.

'That's a good idea', said Mrs. Smith. 'It gets a bit crowded in here when they all come back. Besides, your Father'll be back soon and he'll want a wash. You must excuse us, my dear, but we have to wash in front of the fire in the tin bath. We don't have room upstairs and it's too far to carry the buckets of water. So we all have to make ourselves scarce when the men want to wash. It's not ideal, but we manage. You must think us very strange. You're not from round here, are you?'

'Er… no… Mrs. Smith. I can't really explain how I got here and, if I did try, I'm not sure it would make any sense. I don't really understand it myself. But I'm very grateful to Tom for rescuing me and to you for the lovely meal.'

'Don't mention it, my dear. You're very welcome. It's not very often Tom brings a friend home. And you speak so nicely too. You must excuse Tom. He tries to copy the boys at school. He didn't always drop his aitches, you know. I think he does it to be the same as the other boys. Some of the boys come from Gornal and that's the way they talk. I keep telling him not to, but it makes no difference. Anyway, I must get on. I'll have the others coming in for tea.'

Mrs. Smith sighs, smoothes her hair back into the bun and turns back to her cooking.

'Are yer' ready then?' asks Tom.

'Well, yes, I'd love to go for a walk, but don't you think I'll look rather odd in these clothes?' I said, looking down at my school uniform.

'I'll see what I can find,' said Tom and he disappears up the narrow, steep stairs. It didn't take him long to find a pair of rough woollen trousers, a waistcoat, and a flat cap.

'Put these on. They were my brother's. They might be a bit big, but they'll do. Yer can put 'em on in the wash-'ouse out the back. You can't miss it.'

The washhouse is a small brick building at the back of the cottage, across a tiny yard. In the corner of the room is a big copper bowl. It must be where Mrs. Smith does the washing. Beside the copper stands an iron mangle and something called a washing dolly. I've seen a picture of it in a book. It's used to pound the clothes up and down in the copper to get the dirt out.

I struggle into the trousers. They're supposed to be knee-length breeches, but they're long on me. They're rather rough and itchy too. I must look stupid, but hopefully, no one's going to see me. And in any case no one knows me here, do they? Back in the cottage Tom is ready to go.

'Don't be late, you two. Remember it's school in the morning and your Dad doesn't like you out late on a school day,' said Mrs. Smith. 'Mind what you're up to, Tom, and look after your friend.'

'I will, Mom, don't fret,' said Tom, anxious to get out of the door. 'Come on then, Bella. We'll 'ave to get a move on. Yer best keep up.' Tom starts walking so quickly I'm having a hard job to keep up with him. We're walking past more fields and trees. There's lots of farmland all around us and I can't see many houses.

Along the lane, we come to a high wall. It must mark the boundary to someone's land. Before I have time to ask, Tom pulls me down behind the wall.

'Watch out. Mr. Bradley's outside by 'is barn.'

'Well, he can't stop us walking by, can he? We're not doing any harm.'

'Just do as I says. 'E don't like me, see. We best wait 'til 'e's gone.' I'm glad I'm wearing the old trousers because the lane is muddy. I hope Mrs. Smith won't mind too much if they get dirty.

Tom pops his head over the top of the wall. 'It's all clear. 'E's gone back in the'ouse. Now 'ow are yer on climbin' walls?'

'I think I can manage. But I thought we were just going for a walk.'

'Listen 'ere, there's no point goin' walkin' if yer don't get somat on the way.'

'What exactly are we getting, Tom?'

27

'The thing is, Mr. Bradley's got a good many fruit trees. Well.. 'e can't eat all the fruit 'iself, can 'e? So I'm sort of 'elpin' 'im out, see.'

'You mean to say that we're going scrumping?'

'That's right. You ain't slow, are yer?'

'I'm sorry to tell you, Tom, but even though you've been very kind to me, you're not getting me to steal apples.'

'It ain't exackly stealin', though, is it? I mean, 'e's got too much stuff an' it'll ony gus bad. Now that seems wrong to my way o' thinkin'. It's a sin to let it all rot. We'm only 'elpin. But if yum frit, forget it.'

I can tell that Tom is cross with me. What do I do? I know that stealing is wrong, but Tom has so little and, if the fruit is going to waste, it's not so bad, is it? And anyway, I'm not frit, I mean frightened. I'll show him that I can be brave. He thinks I'm just another feeble girl. I can do anything he can. I'll show him.

'Right then,' I said, indignantly. 'Let's go. I just hope we don't get caught. Your mother won't be too pleased.'

'Yer right, she won't. If I gets caught agen, I'm for the 'igh jump.'

'You mean you've been caught before?'

'Only wunce. But round 'ere, if yer gets caught a second time, you can get sent to jail.'

'But that's not possible, surely? You're only a child.'

'Oh, but I can. I 'eard of a boy, ony eight years old,'e was flogged and locked in prison for stealing a few plums. And another time, a thirteen year old girl was caught pinchin' apples from a garden and she got sent to prison. Mind yer, there was such a fuss med about it, they sent 'er to Reform school for four years instead.' I gulped. How can a child be sent to prison?

'Mind, there's plenty of other punishments. Some kids caught stealin' get sent to Australia, so they says, on a big ship. A boy, in London, got sent an 'e woz ony eight, same as me.' This is frightening. I know stealing is against the law, but it does seem rather harsh, sending young children to prison or transporting them to Australia.

'We better make sure we don't get caught then, Tom. Come on. What are we waiting for?'

Chapter 5.

Tom's right. Mr. Bradley has got loads of fruit trees. There are stacks of apples lying on the ground. I can easily pick some up, but I wish I'd got a bag or something to carry them in. Tom says to put them in the pockets of these trousers, but they'll be full in no time. Tom's busy climbing a few of the trees to get the bigger apples, but really there's no need. I think he just likes to climb trees and it's an excuse.

I have to be careful though, because some of the apples look delicious, until I turn them over and find that the worms have got there first. Why do they always seem to pick the biggest and juiciest looking ones?

I'm happily picking up the apples and stuffing them inside the woolly waistcoat and I nearly didn't hear Tom signal to me.

'Look out! Mr. Bradley's coming!' With that, Tom jumps down from the trees and starts to run towards the wall.

'Come on! Quick let's go! Follow me.' I'm not as fast as Tom, but I know that I've got to reach the wall and climb over before Mr. Bradley sees me or we'll both be in big trouble, especially Tom.

I scramble over dead branches and sting myself on nettles. I'm dropping apples out of the waistcoat as I go. Oh dear, I'm leaving a trail of evidence, but I can't stop to pick them up. I've nearly reached the wall when I hear a loud, angry voice behind me.

'Stop! Stop! You varmints, you! Wait 'til I get my hands on you, you little beggars. It's no use you hidin'. I know it's you, Tom Smith. You just wait. You're for the 'igh jump this time, I can tell you. It's the magistrates for you, this time.'

Fortunately for us, Mr. Bradley is a big heavy man and he can't run as fast as we can. I might reach the wall before him, but I've got to get over it. I think Tom has already climbed over. I only hope he's waiting for me on the other side.

My legs are aching and my heart is banging in my chest. I bet Mr. Bradley can hear it. I've got to keep going, but the weight of the apples filling my pockets is slowing me down. I daren't throw them away. Not only will they give Mr. Bradley the proof he needs, but we'll be going home empty handed and we'll both be in trouble for nothing. At least this way, Tom and his family will be able to enjoy some nice juicy apples. But, thinking about it, if Tom's sent to Australia, they won't be much use to him, will they?

I mustn't let too much thinking slow me down. A great deal relies on me getting out of Mr. Bradley's orchard.

By the time I reach the wall, my clothes are sticking to me. I'm out of breath and very hot, but I'm more afraid than anything else. I don't want to be responsible for Tom going to jail, or Australia.

Suddenly, I hear Tom's voice from the other side of the wall. 'Quick... over here... there's some foot-holes.' I'm relieved to hear Tom's voice, but I can hear Mr. Bradley shouting close behind me. I put one foot up and manage to get a grip on one stone. Can I lever myself up to the next stone? It's easy for Tom. He's got longer legs than me and he's done this stacks of times before.

I'm scraping my knees against the rough stone and I've broken three or four fingernails. My hands are sore from hanging on, but I've got to push myself up somehow. Yes! I've got another foot-hole... if I can just pull myself up. I'll never lift all this weight, the heavy woollen clothes and the pockets full of apples, never mind my own weight. It would be so much easier to fall back and give myself up. But I must think about Tom. I'll probably get away with a telling off or even a beating, but, for Tom, the consequences are far more serious.

This thought gives me a bit more strength and with one enormous push, I grab the top of the wall with my fingers. Tom's head appears and he grabs me with both hands. He gives a mighty pull and I end up in a crumpled heap at the bottom of the wall.

I want to stop to my breath back, but Tom says we must run. He grabs my hand again and we head back up the lane. My legs feel like jelly, but the mushy mess of squashed apples bouncing up and down inside the waistcoat reminds me that I must get a move on for Tom's sake, as well as my own. How we manage to reach Tom's cottage without collapsing, I don't know, but we stagger into the wash-house before any of the family hear us.

'Thank goodness we're safe now,' I said to Tom, hardly able to breath. 'Don't you believe it. He knows it was me. He'll be coming after me, just you wait and see.'

'Well, how will he find us?'

'He'll find a way. I wouldn't be surprised if he doesn't turn up at school tomorrow to tell Willerby, he'll love any chance to report me, after he's given me a good beating. He's mean and cruel and he hates me.'

'Do we have to go to school tomorrow, then? Why don't we just pretend to go and hide out for the day? I know some of the boys at our school do that.'

'There's no way I can do that. I'd be in more trouble. My Mum has to pay for me to go to school, so I'd feel I'd let her down.

Besides, I'm more scared of my Mum than anything. You want to feel the back of her hand. The others say the same, it's not just me. She's the boss. One word from her and we all jump.'

'Tom, I've noticed something... you're talking properly. Your mother will be pleased.'

'I don't think she'll be pleased no matter how I talk, when she finds out what I've done. Anyway, we best get some sleep. You can sleep upstairs with the girls and I'll sleep down here in the kitchen. I hope you don't mind sharing. My sister will find you something to sleep in. We need some rest to face the music, as they say, tomorrow.'

'I'll say 'goodnight' then, Tom. I have to say, whatever happens tomorrow, it was really exciting and great fun, just a pity we got caught.'

Chapter 6

I open my eyes and look around. I forget where I am, until I see Tom's older sister, Emma, sleeping beside me. Between us, I find a small pair of feet. They must belong to Alice. Obviously the girls sleep in one bedroom and the boys sleep in the other room. But that can't be right... where do Mr. and Mrs. Smith sleep? And where were the boys sleeping last night? It must be that Mrs. Smith and the two girls sleep in one bedroom and, somehow, all the men sleep in the other room. They must have had a change round just for my benefit. That was so kind of them.

I can't imagine my brother, Tom, giving up his bed for a stranger. He moans when I even knock on his door and he hates Mum cleaning his room. He says she's messing with his stuff. I don't think she does. And anyway, he hasn't got anything important in there. I sneaked in one time and had a look round. He doesn't know, he'd kill me if he found out.

It makes me feel very strange to think that this lovely family, who don't have very much, are being so nice to me. I wish I could do something for them. Instead, I've helped Tom to get into really serious trouble. I wish Gran was here, she'd tell me what to do. I do miss her. It makes me sad to think that I might not see her again. I've no idea how I'll get back home, or if I ever will.

Suddenly, I hear a voice calling upstairs. It's Mrs. Smith. 'Come on, you children. It's time to get up. You'll be late for school and work.'

A sleepy Alice crawls out from under the bedclothes and looks at me suspiciously.

'It's alright, Alice. Your mother knows I'm here. We better get dressed and go downstairs. Tom and I have to go to school. I don't suppose you're old enough to go school yet, are you?'

'She'll have to go next year, ' said Emma. 'The twins are five, but Mom can't afford to pay for all three of them and anyway, next year Tom will have to go to work, he'll be nine,' said Emma.

While we are getting dressed, Alice says nothing, but stares at me. I don't think she likes me much, but I can't say I blame her. I mean how would you feel if a complete stranger came to your house and slept in your bed?

'Get a move on, Alice. Mom will have the tea brewing,' said Emma, sharply. She must have noticed the unfriendly way Alice was looking at me, because she added: 'Don't take any notice of Alice, she's always in a sulk. Mom says that one of her looks'll turn the milk sour. It's not just you, she's like it with everyone. Dad's the only one who can get her to smile and that's not very often. It's usually when he's drunk and he's brought her something 'cos he feels guilty. Anyway, we best get downstairs ourselves.'

I put my own school uniform on. It looks a bit crumpled and out of place here, but I don't think it's a good idea to wear the woolly breeches I wore last night, especially if Mr. Bradley does come to school looking for us. The grass stains and the holes in the knees might just give us away.

Downstairs, Mrs. Smith had made some tea and there were several chunks of bread on the table.

'It's not much I'm afraid. We've got some bacon, but I'm keeping it for The Wake. Did Tom tell you about it?'

'Yes, he did. It sounds good fun. I wish I could be here to see it.' As soon as I'd said it, I realised it was a mistake. How can I explain to Mrs. Smith who's been so very kind to me that I really want to go back home?

'Oh dear, are you going so soon? You know you're welcome to stay as long as you like, but I suppose your family will be wondering about you,' I wonder. I'm sure Gran will be missing me. She likes me to help her, especially when she's making one of her dresses or hats, but as for the others? I'm not too sure. Mum will be busy dreaming up one of her fantastic recipes. Dad will be too busy with his inventions. As for Tom, he'll just be happy that he's got rid of me. He thinks I'm a boring girl and a nuisance. That's alright, 'cos I think he's horrid anyway. But I do miss my home, especially Gran. I'm trying to think what to say to Mrs. Smith, when Tom comes in.

'We best get a move on, Bella. We mustn't make Willerby mad, must we?' said Tom, giving me a knowing look.

'Er.. no.. you're right. I'll just finish this tea and then we'll go. Where are your other brothers this morning?'

'Oh, they went to work at five. They 'as to be up at the estate by 'alf past, or they 'as their pay docked. I 'spect Dad's still a'bed, isn't 'e Mom?'

'Well, yes, but your father's got a lot to do. He's got a last lot of nails to finish before the Wake. I shall get Alice and Henry to help him later.'

'Aren't they young to be working with nails?' I ask.

'Don't fret, they'll be quite safe. We don't let them get too close to the presses. They just help with the sorting and polishing, then, when they're ready, Tom takes them to the nail shop when he gets home from school, don't you Tom?'

'Yes, Mom. We must be off now, mustn't be late,' said Tom, nervously. I can tell what he's thinking. He's just hoping that he will be home after school and not sent before the magistrate and locked up.

I find my school bag and pack away the pieces of bread and cheese that Mrs. Smith wrapped in a piece of muslin for our lunch. I know Tom is anxious to be gone, so I say 'goodbye' quickly.

'Thank you so very much for having me and letting me stay, Mrs. Smith. It was very kind of you.'

'Don't mention it, my dear. You're very welcome. Come back with Tom tonight, if you'd like to, but I don't want to interfere. Your parents may be expecting you. I must say it's lovely to meet such a nice friend of Tom's.' To my surprise, she put her arms around me and gave me a slight kiss on the cheek.

'You're such a good influence on him, I'm sure, not like those boys who are always getting him into trouble. Take care then and off you go.'

As soon as we're out of the door, I feel a heavy, sickly feeling. I think they call it feeling guilty. Mrs. Smith thinks I'm a good influence on her son. If only she knew...

'Come on, we best 'face the music' as they say,' said Tom.

'I don't know why they say that, I can't hear anyone singing, can you?' Secretly, I'm imagining the swish of Mr. Willerby's cane.

Chapter 7

Tom doesn't say much on the walk to school. I know he's worried in case Mr. Willerby knows about last night. I just hope Mr. Bradley won't be able to prove it was us, so he won't do anything.

As we get nearer to school, Tom says 'hello' to some of the other children, who mostly stare at me. One or two of the girls give me embarrassed smiles. They probably recognise me from yesterday's drill session. I was the one with the bright red face.

When we reach the schoolyard, Tom has to go into the boys' part and I have to go with the girls. It all seems peculiar because we all meet up in the classroom. I suppose it's because there aren't many classes, just one for the very young children, taught by a monitor and one for the rest taught by Mr. Willerby, worse luck.

Suddenly, one of the monitors comes out carrying a big school bell. She stands by the entrance and gives the bell a big shake. A loud clanging noise echoes around the yard and all the girls move to make a line by the big front door. I follow them into the classroom. This time I find a desk in the girls' line. I can see Tom across the room, but he's not too keen to acknowledge me. We all stand behind our seats in silence, waiting.

All too soon, the door is pushed open and, in a flurry of black gown, Mr. Willerby appears. Unfortunately, he's still wearing that miserable expression, as if he's got a nasty smell under his nose. I can almost feel everyone shaking in their boots, afraid to do something wrong. I bet Tom's feeling nervous, I know I am.

'Good morning, class,' said Mr. Willerby, in a stern voice. I'm sure he doesn't wish anyone a good morning, really. I wonder if there's a Mrs. Willerby? I feel sorry for her, if there is.

'Good morning, Mr. Will... er... by,' the children chant and I have to join in.

'Sit! And no noise!' He gives the command and everyone sits at their desk, as quietly as possible, almost afraid to breathe. One of the girls sitting at the front gives out the slates and one of the boys gives out the slate pencils. A slate and a pencil are placed in front of me. I can see a row of sums on the board and I'm just about to pick up the pencil to start, when Tom sees me. He gives a loud cough and shakes his head. I immediately put down the pencil and fold my hands under the desk, like the others are doing. Phew. Tom has saved me from the wrath of Mr. Willerby again. Once the slates and pencils are given out, we all sit waiting.

'Tables,' orders Mr. Willerby, and at once the children begin reciting the two-times table.

41

Fortunately, I actually know my tables, so I don't feel too unhappy about this command. Sadly, the boy named Jenkins isn't so sure. Mr. Willerby spots him out of the corner of his cold, beady eye and yells out his name.

'Jenkins! Come here at once!' Everyone stops reciting and seems to shudder. They know what's coming next.

'Jenkins! The stool! At this minute!' Poor Jenkins. He begins to shake. He's a weak little boy and his clothes are thin and worn. Timidly, he gets up from his seat and obeys. He climbs on to the stool and Mr. Willerby places a pointed hat on his head. It reads STUPID in large black letters. I can't believe anyone can be so cruel. Thank goodness it doesn't happen at my school. I often get things wrong. I'd be wearing the hat more than anyone else!

The rest of the class look down at their slates and, on Mr. Willerby's command, busy themselves with the sums on the board. There is silence. I wonder how long poor Jenkins has to stand on the stool. I'm still wondering when the classroom door bursts open and in storms Mr. Bradley, looking extremely angry.

'Excuse me Headmaster, but where is 'e?'

'To whom do you refer, Mr. Bradley? How may I assist you?'

'It's that varmint Smith and his mate I'm a-looking for. I know 'e's 'ere somewhere.'

'Well, if you can tell me the nature of his offence, I'm sure I can deal with it appropriately. I must remind you, Mr. Bradley, that this is my school and I'm in charge here and you are out of order.'

'Don't come talking to me with all them fancy words. I know my rights and I shall ,ave 'em.'

I can see that Mr. Willerby is cross with Mr. Bradley for questioning his authority. Perhaps he'll just send him on his way. That way we might just get away with it. I daren't look across at Tom. He's keeping his head down so that Mr. Bradley won't recognise him. I better do the same.

'If you'll just explain your grievance, Mr. Bradley, perhaps I can help you. What seems to be the problem?'

'It's that Tom Smith, he's bin scrumpin' my apples agen and I'm not 'avin'it. You 'ear me. It's not the first time 'e's done it. It's the law for 'im this time, and the little lad with 'im. I don't know 'is name but I'll know 'im agen if I saw him'

'I can understand your anger, Mr. Bradley, but perhaps, if I may suggest, once you've identified the culprits, you'll allow me to decide their punishment.'

Mr. Bradley seems unsure about this, but he knows he must have Mr. Willerby's permission to look around the class. I'm not sure what is worse, being brought before the law, or being punished by Mr. Willerby.

'Very well, then Headmaster, but you see as 'ow they're proper punished, understand me. 'Cos if 'e gets away with it this time, I'll bring the law on 'im meself, sure I will.'

'Mr. Bradley, I can assure you that the perpetrators of this crime will be brought to justice and will be severely punished.

'Right then,' grunted Mr. Bradley begrudgingly, 'if you're sure they'll get what they deserve, I'll bid you 'good day'. With that, Mr. Bradley puts on his flat cap and walks out of the room.

Mr. Willerby turns to us. We all hold our breath. 'Pencils down! You all heard Mr. Bradley. Has anyone anything to say? Smith! Stand up!'

44

Tom gets up out of his seat. I can see he's shaking. I'm shaking too.

'Come here, boy!'

Tom walks meekly to the front of the class.

Have you anything to say, Smith?'

'Please sir, no sir,' whispers Tom.

'Do you admit your crime?'

'Please sir, yes sir.'

'Well, I suppose that's something,' boomed Mr. Willerby,' at least you have the decency to admit it and not try to lie your way out of it. Tell me, did you commit this crime on your own, or did you have an accomplice? Speak up now.'

I'm holding my breath. Will Tom give me away? But if he doesn't, I can't let him take all the blame, can I?

'Please sir, no sir. I was on my own, sir. Mr. Bradley was mistaken, sir.'

Bless Tom. What a kind and brave boy he is. But I can't let him do this. I must take my share of the blame, whatever the punishment.

There's a stillness in the classroom. Mr. Willerby is obviously wondering how to deal with Tom. I must be brave too and own up.

Slowly, I get up out of my seat. The children turn to stare at me. No one gets out of their seat unless Mr. Willerby tells them to.

'Please sir.' My voice is rather trembly.' Please sir, I was with Tom, sir. I was the other thief.'

Mr. Willerby wasn't quite sure where the voice was coming from. I'm not very tall and I'm standing at the back of the class.

'Who said that? Come here, boy, come here at once!'

Feeling very wobbly at the knees, I manage to walk between the rows of desks to stand in front of Mr. Willerby.

'What have we here? Did I hear you correctly, girl?'

'Yes sir, you did. I was with Tom. It was my fault, sir. I asked him to take me,' I lied. Well, it was the least I could do.

'Your name, girl?'

'Arabella, sir, Arabella Twigg.'

SIR', he bellowed. 'Well, Miss Arabella Twigg, it seems you are anxious to take responsibility for this crime. Are you telling me that Tom Smith was an unwilling accomplice?'

'Yes, sir, that's right, sir. Tom's not to blame, sir. Please don't punish him.'

'I must say I find this difficult to believe, but if you're certain that you are the main culprit, I must take your word for it.'

Tom looks at me in amazement and is about to say something, so I quickly, say 'Yes, sir, please, sir. It was definitely my fault, sir.'

'Very well, but I hope you realise this is a very serious matter. Go to my study and wait there. I will be along presently to decide on an appropriate punishment. This is your first offence of this nature, I trust.'

'Yes, sir.'

'Go along then and await my decision.' I have one last look at Tom. I'm sure he was mouthing the words 'thank you' and his eyes look a bit watery.

'Take her to my room,' he orders one of the boys at the front. Meekly I leave the room and follow the boy along the dark corridor. Very little light ever shines inside this building. The gloom seems to match how I'm feeling. I know Mr. Willerby won't make any allowances for me, even if I am a girl. I think he actually enjoys punishing children. He's nothing but a big bully really. I'm glad we don't have teachers like him in my school. Thinking about my school makes me feel very sad and a bit tearful. I wonder what Eloise is doing. I suppose she's not my friend anymore. Still, I can't blame her if I just disappeared and never told her.

We reach Mr. Willerby's study and the boy opens the door for me. I can tell he's not going to hang around to keep me company, so I whisper my thanks and go inside. The room is lighter than I expected and full of books. A big wooden desk fills the middle of the room and one of those wooden chairs with rounded arms stands behind it. That must be where Mr. Willerby writes his reports.

I don't know whether to sit on the other small wooden chair in the corner or stand and wait in front of the desk. Perhaps standing up will look better. I'm not feeling very brave. In fact, I'm absolutely terrified. I don't know what I'm most afraid of, fear of pain if he gives me the cane, or fear of what else he might do. I remember feeling like this once before. It was when I went to see Gran in her little house and I kept knocking on the door and she didn't answer. I was certain something terrible had happened to her. I was really scared. It's when you don't know what's going to happen that things are most scary, isn't it?

It's all very quiet and I've been standing here for ages. Perhaps he's forgotten all about me.

Just then, the door bangs open. Oh no, this is it. What is he going to do to me? I daren't turn round. I'm keeping my eyes tightly shut and try to stop shaking.

'Arabella? What are you doing here?' I hear a voice. But it's not Mr. Willerby. Who is it?

'Arabella, what are doing in here? Has someone sent you on an errand? I don't remember asking to see you, did I? I know you've been rather late a few times lately, but I'm prepared to overlook that.'

I know that voice. It's Mrs. Osborne, my own class teacher. I turn around and there she is, struggling with a pile of books. That's why the door banged.

'Oh, Mrs. Osborne, you don't know how pleased I am to see you. Let me help you with you books. You see, I didn't really want to get tom into trouble. After all, his family had been so kind to me and everything. And I know he'll be sent to prison if he gets caught again and he's such a kind boy and they haven't any money, but they were happy to share everything with me...'

'Stop, Arabella. Just stop and take a deep breath. I really haven't the faintest idea what you're talking about. Look, help me with these books and then you can explain everything to me properly.'

'Oh, yes, of course. I'm so sorry. It's just that I'm so pleased to see you. You can't imagine.'

'Arabella, what are you talking about? I was in the classroom with you, not fifteen minutes ago. I sent you out to the store room for some new exercise books remember?'

Remember? How could I remember when so much has happened to me? I don't suppose Mrs. Osborne's going to believe me anyway. I'm not sure that I believe it myself.

'Hand me those books, please Arabella, would you?' Her question makes me jump. I pick up the pile of books and hand them to her. She looks down at my hands.

'Arabella, what have you done to your hands? You've got big red marks across your palms. It looks as if someone has hit them with a stick. I do hope they aren't sore.'

I don't like to say anything, but I can't help thinking that my hands didn't hurt half as much as another certain part would, if Mr. Willerby had caught up with me.

P.S. I don't suppose you believe me either, do you?

Printed in Great
Britain
by Amazon